ALPHA'S SHY OMEGA

MPREG Wolf Shifter Romance

Michael Levi

ISBN: 9798356202780
Imprint: Independently published

1st edition

CONTENTS

CHAPTER 1

I was shy, no denying it, I thought while pulling up my backpack straps. Moving down the hallway, I soon found myself turning my head to the left and encountering an imposing, mouthwatering presence standing close to the front gate.

Being one of the guards, he was well known on campus. He was also always cheery and cracking jokes, always looking so confident in what he could do.

Everyone fawned over him and that was putting it mildly, I thought before walking with quick, short steps toward the gate. With my head lowered, I was hoping that he wasn't going to notice me. Carwel always did, so it wouldn't be surprising if it happened again, but for the love of God, he couldn't notice me going out through the gate.

And yet, I couldn't stop doing the one thing that was the biggest, single mistake that I kept on doing, which was to steal glances at him. Those mesmerizing, jaw-dropping muscles, the stubble on his face, and his plump, attention-drawing lips... How could I be looking anywhere else right now?

There was just something different about him, something I couldn't put my finger on, but which kept drawing me to him, making me think that we could be something together, but realizing that such a thing was just impossible.

I didn't hope for anything, I thought while realizing that I was approaching him. Being in an ocean of students, I knew that he had no reason to notice me among them, but sometimes, he still did.

Increasing my pace, I was now no more than some feet from him before realizing that he just turned his eyes in my direction. Uh-oh, I thought before stopping in my tracks and someone bumped hard into me.

My backpack fell from me, the contents inside of it spilling out. Shit, I thought before going down on my knees right away. My cheeks flushing red, I just hoped that Carwel wasn't going to notice me looking like a fool while fumbling to pick back up my stuff and shove it into my backpack.

"Why is this happening to me?" I asked myself while cursing everything that always happened in my life, wishing that the ground would just swallow me whole.

After shoving my pencil case into my backpack and everyone laughed at me, Carwel made his way through the crowd. Everyone was gathering around me, so it was quite difficult for him to find me.

When I realized that he was no more than a couple of feet from me, I froze up. I didn't think that we were going to interact after the last time. I thought that last time had been enough to destroy whatever reputation I had with him, but it appeared that the fates still wanted to fuck my life a little more.

"Sorry. I'm almost finished with this. I'm so pathetic," I mumbled, wishing that he didn't hear anything, but knowing that he probably still did. This biker guard was more than that to me. He was also my crush, and every time that he was close to me, I felt goosebumps in my body, like now.

"Here. Let me help you with this," he said before grabbing my backpack and lifting it up, positioning himself behind me to make sure that it wasn't going to fall from me next time.

Still blushing, I said, "thanks." And after saying that, I realized that everyone that had gathered around me was already dispersing. I supposed that thanks to Carwel being focused on me while the other guards took charge of the gate, everybody realized that they couldn't bully me right now – at least, not without drawing out his wrath. "But you really didn't need to do this. I was already finishing this. I have no idea why I stopped while everyone was rushing out of campus. I'm so dumb."

He shook his head, putting his hands on his waist. "One day, you're going to have to realize that you aren't like you think you are. You're actually pretty nice and I'm sure that you have a golden heart."

Still blushing, I didn't know what to do, so I just said, "thanks." After rubbing the back of my head, I had no idea what to do and what to say. Everything was such a whirlwind after I began to get used to the fact that we were interacting again.

"Well, good luck. Don't get yourself lost while going back home, okay?" He said before going back to standing in his spot by the gate. After that, I just went outside relief washing over me after realizing that we didn't have to interact anymore and that Carwel had been pretty nice to me, as he always was.

I didn't know why it was always like this, but he was always so nice to me. Still, I was pretty sure that there was nothing behind it that I didn't already know. It wasn't like he was looking for a relationship or anything like that. In fact, the last time that I overheard him talking about something that resembled him being in a relationship, he said that he wasn't looking for anyone in particular, other than the true one.

He said that he was still waiting for his fated mate, especially after trying with so many Omegas and all of them being disappointments.

I had a car, so at least I didn't have to interact with anyone anymore today. Some of the college students took the bus to go back to their homes, but not me.

I didn't have loving parents, but they gave me this car. It was nothing for them. It was pretty cheap, considering how much money they made and how much of it was in their bank accounts, I thought before gripping the steering wheel and accelerating. After that, it was pretty easy for me to arrive at my home, pulling up before going out and checking the sides of the property to make sure that there was nobody around.

Sometimes, there were surprises with that, and right now I didn't want to be surprised. Being an introvert, I always felt overwhelmed by spending too much time with other people, and now was no different, I thought before opening the front door, falling onto the couch, and then turning on the TV.

After that encounter with Carwel, I needed to wind down, I thought before locking my eyes on the TV and not thinking about anything, especially Carwel.

He was hot and all, but I was very sure that we couldn't be fated mates, especially after all the times that I made a fool of myself in front of him.

CHAPTER 2

Carwel

Walking behind the window, the last thing I thought I was going to see was him sitting at the table, his hand jotting down something on the paper. Nokon was a student, so it wasn't surprising that he was attending a class right now. What was surprising was that I was watching him from afar, my cock jumping under my pants.

Gosh, what the hell was I thinking? I asked myself, taking a step away from there, but realizing that I actually found myself glued to the spot behind the window where I was.

The truth was that I really found him cute, even if also too shy, I thought before remembering that I was 30 years old, so even if there was something between us, it couldn't actually happen, not without people judging us.

I knew what they would be talking about if they found out that we were in a relationship. They would think that I was some kind of sexual predator. Being a biker was nice and all, but I just didn't want to lose this job as a front gate guard. It composed a good portion of my income, and it really couldn't be any different. Considering the rising crime rates around here, institutions like this college sought more and more people like me to keep them protected, including the students.

I shook my head, taking another step away from the window,

but not before noticing that Nokon had straightened up his spine after the professor asked him a question. I was unable to make out what it was, but I still wished I could be there to help him with that, even though chances were that I wouldn't be able to do anything about that.

His hair, his lips, his nose, his eyes, and pretty much everything that composed how he looked made me feel something alien, something that I shouldn't be feeling for someone so much younger.

Not to mention that his life was completely different from mine. At best, we could date and have a one-night stand, but it would be nothing more than that, I thought before checking to make sure that my pistol was still in my waist.

It still was, I thought before finally moving away from the window, though not without stopping again and finding out that something massive was going on in the class. Something that hurt my heart in an instant, I thought before rushing into the building and looking for him. No matter what was going on here now, I was going to help Nokon.

Nokon sat on a bench, burying his head in his hands. After throwing his eyes in my direction the moment when he noticed that I was coming, though, he straightened up his spine and tried to hide his crying, but it was too late for him, I thought while trying to hide the smile that crept up my face. I shouldn't be smiling, especially after finding out that he was going through a moment of distress.

Putting his backpack on, he attempted to move away from me, but then he stopped when I did the same. He realized that he couldn't escape from me. I was worried about him, so I was going to ask as many questions as I could without making this too weird.

"Something going on?" I asked, stepping toward him. He didn't immediately step away from me, which was a positive.

"No, I was just freaking out about something that actually doesn't even make sense. It's just that there is this one thing in the class that I couldn't understand at all, and then I began to get desperate, and then I started to feel sorry for myself, and then I…

Then, you know everything that happened, so now you can make fun of me, just like everyone."

After that, I chuckled. Nokon really looked so cute and sweet, stumbling with his words. "You don't really need to feel sorry for yourself. If you need an ear to talk about this, I'm here."

His eyes widened in an instant. "You?" He asked, finding it unbelievable. He should be finding it like that, especially considering that we actually didn't have anything in common other than the few times we talked. "You actually care about me?"

How silly Nokon was being, I thought, stepping toward him before finding myself no more than some inches from him. After that, I pointed with my chin toward a spot on campus where we could have more privacy. It was right outside, by one of the walls of the building, where we could talk about whatever it was that was bothering him without anyone bothering us.

He nodded and we went there. There was this bench where we sat. I put my hands between my legs, hunching over slightly. With my eyes focused on him, I asked, "do you want to talk a little bit more about that?"

He sighed, running his fingers through his hair. "I've always really thought that I'm good at math, but after the first few classes in that course I'm taking, I realized that I'm actually not really that good and that I was only imagining that I was. That's why I feel so bad about it, especially given that my family, even though we are rich, would never help me any more than they already have. I'm all on my own here," he said, still blushing.

And in the meantime, I couldn't help but feel connected to him. That was genuinely something that he was struggling with, and I wanted to help. I did go to college once, Civil Engineering, so maybe there were some things that I learned I could teach him.

CHAPTER 3

Carwel

"I see. That's a pretty common thing to be struggling with. When you are in college, things are very different, especially dating and finding the right partner. It's around this time that you begin to think you will find your fated mate."

His eyes widened, most likely thinking something that he couldn't say right now, not without making this weird. To be honest, I was supposed to be patrolling the campus and watching for anything that required my attention, but right now I just didn't want to go anywhere away from Nokon.

I knew that this moment was all about his cuteness and how sweet he was, but I still couldn't stop my eyes from moving up and down, scrutinizing every part of his body, wishing to see him naked and melting under me.

Gosh, what was even happening to me? Again, I was about 10 years older than him and whatever could happen between us, it would be weird. Not to mention that if he ever found himself in the kind of environment where I was from, he would certainly feel out of place and wish that he never got involved with me. On top of that, the different power dynamics between us meant that I didn't want to feel like I was taking advantage of him.

"I know. I haven't even begun to think about who my fated mate could be. To be honest, I don't think that he's around here, attending this college. There are so many people in the world and he could be anywhere. The more I think about it, the more I realize that my possible fated mate is probably somewhere else I can't even reach."

"You don't have to think about it that way," I thought, remembering that, if it ever happened to me, I wouldn't know until it couldn't be changed. The moment I found my fated mate, I would just know.

"Maybe that person could be me," I said, just throwing that out there as though I was fishing for his reaction. And, when his eyes widened and he blushed even harder than before, I knew that I'd gotten him.

"I don't think that it's you. You are nice and all, Carwel, but we can't really be for each other. I mean, you are so different from me. You work as a guard here and I imagine that you are going to continue working here for the time being, while I'll probably find myself working somewhere completely different, and then there I might find my fated mate."

"Well, that might be right, but..." After taking a deep breath and noticing that his leg was getting closer to mine, which was something that he wasn't doing anything about, much less stopping it from continuing, I said, "so, going back to what you said about needing help with a certain math problem... Do you wanna show me which one it is?"

His eyes widened again, showing me that he didn't think that I was going to ask something like that. And truly, I wouldn't have had, considering that I shouldn't continue interacting with him.

For now, there was nothing weird with that yet, even though it was beginning to get considerably harder to hide my semi right now.

Even the fur on my body was beginning to show.

But it wasn't like this Omega wasn't showing me some of the signs that I was looking for, either, of course.

His pupils were still dilated. There was something about me that he thought, something that he couldn't let out – not yet, anyway, and without compromising who he was in this college.

"You think that you can help me with it? I mean, I don't want to offend you, but the last thing one would think about you is if you actually know much about math."

"I actually do know a little bit about it. You don't know this, and really, you don't have to, considering that I just don't look like it, but I've had some Civil Engineering classes before. That is, until I dropped out."

There was a moment of silence, Nokon probably wondering why I dropped out. But Nokon was an introvert and shy, so I didn't think that he was going to ask any questions about that.

"Oh, right. The math problem," he said, opening his backpack and taking the notebook out of it. After that, he showed me the page where he was having a little bit of difficulty with the math problem.

After reading it, I scratched my forehead, not because I thought I didn't know how to solve it, but because it was going to take a little bit of time. I took his notebook from his hands and stood up, walking around a single point. Nokon remained seated on the bench where he was, his eyes looking at me and probably wondering what exactly I was doing right now.

Holding up my hand, I said, "don't worry about this. I think I actually know how to solve this problem," I said before sitting back down on the bench and beginning my explanation.

It was actually pretty easy, especially for a Calculus problem. After the explanation was given to him, he looked at me with wonder, his eyes almost teary.

His hands trembling slightly while his leg finally touched mine, he said, "thank you so much. My professor tried so many times to hammer that concept into my head, but it just would never get through, but now that you showed me how simple it is, I get it. It's actually done this way, hmm..."

Smiling, we continued to talk a little bit more about some current things happening on campus, the weather, politics, and a little bit about his life, even though he didn't want to share much about it. After that, I waved my hand over my head, bidding him goodbye.

Nokon waved his hand over his head, hurrying away from me before going back to his home. He had a good time with me, I realized after paying attention to his smile and the way that his eyes shone under the sunlight.

So, what was going to happen now? I asked myself. Could I really give ourselves a chance? To be honest, I had always looked for someone that I could care for as much as I loved, and he fit the bill for that, no denying it.

But even though we liked each other, I didn't want to risk my job here in this college, much less my position in the biker club.

The president and the vice president would probably kick me out of it if they learned that I was dating a college student.

CHAPTER 4

Lying on my bed, I couldn't stop thinking about Nikon. After spending so much time alone and wondering what was going to happen next in my life, I always found myself staring at the ceiling and thinking about it, thinking about all the failed relationships I had before now, including all the times I thought I had found my fated mate, only to realize that it was all pointless.

Was I feeling a little hopeless? Sometimes I did, and other times I found myself hopeful, especially now that I was flipping through the different profiles that I found on this dating app. It was called ClickDesire, and after much searching, I found some potential candidates, some people I could imagine myself having a one-night stand with. Still, I didn't want to get my hopes up.

They all showed interest in me by liking all my photos, shooting me message after message, and sometimes asking if I was talking with someone else. I was desired, no denying it, but it was still so difficult for me to go on a date right now, considering that my mind was still focused on someone else. That someone else was, of course, none other than Nikon.

What was he doing right now? I asked myself, my hand going under my pants and grabbing my cock. Giving it a few strokes, I could imagine him going down on me, his lips wrapping around my grand, swirling his tongue around it while focusing on the underside of it, giving me so much pleasure I would probably come in record time, I thought, smiling and chastising myself for thinking something like that about someone so sweet, someone so different from me, someone that was the very definition of a twink.

I took a deep breath, swiping my finger on the screen over and over again, still moving my fingers around my gland, stroking it gently until I stumbled on something I thought I would never find.

It was Nokon's ClickDesire profile, and he was extremely cute. His profile photo showed him smiling, making me want to be in the photo and pinching his cheeks. It was a pity that I couldn't.

This meant that he was looking for a partner, I concluded, refreshing the screen before finding out that his profile was actually gone now.

What the hell? I asked myself, swiping my finger down on the page one more time, wondering what the hell happened, soon finding out that his profile was really gone. Blinking twice in a row, I concluded that I must've probably imagined that it happened.

But at the same time, I wasn't inebriated and I wasn't dreaming either, I noticed when I pinched my own shoulder.

"What's going on here…?" I asked myself, grabbing Mr. Mitch in my hand and looking at his fake, plastic eyes, wondering if he would finally do the one thing I wished he would do one day, which was to answer my questions when I talked to him.

He was a stuffed toy, so there was no way that it would ever happen. He was just a relic from my past when I was still a child. I brought Mr. Mitch with me here, remembering how difficult it was for me to let go of my childhood.

Still, I put the stuffed toy back on the bed, swiping my finger down the screen one more time, wishing that Nokon's profile would show up again.

Just like last time, it was nowhere to be seen, and I couldn't help but wonder what was up with that.

I dropped my phone on the bed, jumping off the bed before going to the bathroom. After thinking about Nokon so much and seeing his profile on ClickDesire, I had to relieve myself, even though I still thought that this was probably the beginning of something I would regret. Again, the difference in our ages was too significant even though it turned me on, I thought to myself, my fingers moving slowly up and down my prick.

Would it really be so bad if we hooked up? I asked myself, my shaft growing harder and bigger, my balls slapping against my hand. Groaning and huffing, I began to cream into the toilet, shooting line after line of my cum into the water.

Still huffing, but slightly less than before, I flushed the water and then closed the lid of the toilet. After that, I went to the sink, washing my hands. Seeing myself in the mirror, I decided to stop whatever was going on.

The president and the vice president of the motorcycle club were right. One day, I would find my fated mate, and then whatever was going on with me and Nokon would be over.

CHAPTER 5

Nokon

My body freezing up right now, I had no idea what I thought I was doing, my hand holding my phone and trembling. Whatever happened, I must have imagined it. No way that the hot biker guard from college had a ClickDesire profile. No way, I thought before reloading the page and finding out that his profile was still there. Deciding to stop this before it was too late, I hid my profile. Really, it was the only thing I could do. The good thing was that I could still see his photos, and they showed him in his underwear. His body was just... Jesus, how could I even put this into words? I asked myself, my hand going under my pants and stroking my shaft.

His body was mouthwatering, the curves, the lines, the shadows, the highlights, and pretty much everything about it seemed just right. I could just imagine myself sliding my hands over the biceps, the shoulders, his thighs, and pretty much every part of him, including his prick. Given the size of his bulge, I knew that it had to be big. My hand would feel tiny in comparison to the thickness and the length of his shaft, I concluded before lowering my pants and going to the bathroom.

Seeing myself in the mirror, I closed my eyes and began to jerk off while thinking about Carwel mounting me and fucking me until he came inside of me, getting me pregnant with his baby, or maybe even many babies, I thought, wishing that it would happen, but knowing that it probably wouldn't.

After cumming into the toilet, I took my phone back into my hands, and then I fell onto the bed, the night outside serene, the crickets chirping. After relieving myself, I felt so much better and as though I could check his profile one more time without freaking out.

I didn't want Carwel to know that I was on the app, considering that we would probably see each other again, especially given that awkward moment when he told me everything that he could about that math problem, including how to solve it. So, he had been in Civil Engineering, something I never thought possible.

Considering that he had been in it, I wondered what else about his life I had no idea about.

I reloaded the page and then I found out that his profile was still up. The only difference now was that he had a change in his profile picture, but all the other photos were still the same. I wondered why that was, I thought, checking his profile one more time and realizing that it showed him with his buddies from the biker club. He was from the Alpha MC, so that was no surprise.

Seeing that environment, the biker club, his friends, and pretty much everything else associated with it, I knew that any relationship with him would be difficult, and I wasn't really imagining it could happen. It just wouldn't.

To be honest, it only made me realize how impossible it was, I thought before clicking on a button on the app, which made my profile online again.

Panicking, I jammed my finger on the screen, trying to do everything possible to hide my profile, but I then realized it was already too late.

Jesus. What the hell was happening? I asked myself, finding this whole thing unbelievable. It was as though the app wanted to show my profile to Nokon, which couldn't be true unless it was sentient.

Biting my bottom lip, I decided to do something I shouldn't.

Since he had already seen my profile, I might as well take the bait. So, without giving it another thought, I swept right on his profile, liking it.

After that, it was as though everything was a snowball going down a hill.

He even sent me a message, which I clicked on immediately.

Should I reply to it? I asked myself, turning off my phone right away. Now that I lived alone and could do anything I wanted, I could technically go out on a date with him and nobody would know anything about it.

And yet, it would still be awkward, considering that his profile showed his age. 30 years old. Even though he was hot and didn't look as old as he was, the age difference was still there and there was nothing I could do about it.

Still, the possibility of hooking up with someone 10 years older than me made my cock so hard right now it was impossible to control it. I had already jerked off and I should be feeling calmer, my urges relieved, but it wasn't what was happening now.

I took a deep breath after turning the phone back on. Carwel must be thinking that something weird was happening to me now. Also, after that moment with him outside of the Engineering Building, we touched our legs. I'd felt shivers of warmth in my entire body then, which was the reason why I ran away.

I just didn't want anyone noticing my semi and thinking that I was a horny mess that couldn't control his urges, even though that was pretty much the case, sometimes anyway.

Carwel: hey, how are you?

That was his message and I didn't know how to reply to it. I wasn't going to, really, I thought, turning off the phone again and putting my hand under the bed before finding my clock. I needed it to wake me up tomorrow morning or else I would miss my classes.

I usually used the phone for that purpose, but not tonight. Tomorrow, I would probably go to college wearing a hoodie. It was the least I could do, not wishing that Carwel saw me.

But even after that, what did I think would happen, that he would never see me again? There wasn't even another exit out of the campus, so it wasn't like there was another choice for me, I thought, finding this whole thing too unbelievable, especially for someone like me, who didn't have the luxury of going through this without affecting my studies.

And also my sleep.

Covering myself with the blanket and staring at the ceiling, I cursed myself. Carwel probably hated me now.

CHAPTER 6

Nokon

Where was he? I asked myself, pulling over the car before checking the front gate of the college, wondering where Carwel was. I didn't see him at the front gate, my hand trembling. To be honest, many things could form the reason why he wasn't at the front gate right now.

And yes, I was thinking that thanks to our failed conversation yesternight, I thought, moving my hands away from the steering wheel and taking my backpack. After that, I walked out of the car and closed the door.

I thought that after looking at the guard post again I would see him standing there, but he was still nowhere to be seen. There were some other guards posted there, but they were people that I didn't know, I thought before beginning to make my way over there.

Just after that, I crossed the entrance to the campus, making my way to the class. Still turning my head left and right, I thought that I would find Carwel standing somewhere on campus, but he was still nowhere to be seen.

How weird, I thought to myself, my hands gripping the backpack's straps while I continued to beeline to my class. It was another Calculus class and, this time, I was going to take what he taught me to solve the next math problems.

At least, that was my plan, I thought before turning to the left and stumbling into someone in the hallway. Flicking my eyes up, I thought that I was going to find another Alpha professor, given his scent, but after wrinkling my nose, I realized that this scent was actually one that I knew well.

My legs trembled, my cock stiffening. Of course that this was none other than Carwel, whose eyes were staring at me with so many questions that he had to ask me.

After all, what happened yesternight had been no dream or nightmare. It had really happened, and now he wanted to ask me why I ghosted him.

After straightening up my posture, I said, "hey, it's you. I'm so sorry that I bumped into you. Don't know what I was doing, really."

There was a moment of silence, his lips looking like a slit. What was going on in his mind right now? I asked myself, rubbing the back of my head while smiling broadly. I was hoping that looking cute was going to be enough to quench his rage.

Being a biker and a guard, I was pretty sure that Carwel wasn't someone that took well to being ghosted.

"We talked last night," he said, his tone showing his seriousness. Uh-oh. I didn't like the direction this was taking, and I could just imagine him punching me right now for ghosting him.

"Yeah, I guess we kinda did. I found you on ClickDesire and… I was only fucking around. I didn't know what I was doing."

"I thought you were going to message me back."

I was going to do that, but again, it would still have been so weird.

Still rubbing the back of my head, I said, "yeah, I meant to do that, but then my phone just stopped working and it broke on me. That's what happened, really. I even took it to the repair shop before coming here."

After giving him that explanation, he shook his head, saying, "hopefully that's true. Given the change in your scent, I feel like you are lying to me. But you are nice and you've always been nice to me, so I don't think that you're really lying."

Phew, I thought, relaxing my posture after hearing his words. If he wasn't going to punch me right now as punishment for ghosting him, then everything was okay, I thought before taking a step to the side. If he was okay with it, then there was nothing else to say, and I could end this awkwardness before it was too late.

After that, he took a step to the side, stopping me. I couldn't help but lock my eyes with his again, imagining that he was only playing with me right now.

He had to be, right? There were people still walking past us, still going to their destinations, and even though nobody was actually paying attention to us, he wouldn't make it so I couldn't walk past him, right?

But his eyes were still staring at me fiercely, his lips still becoming like a slit. What the hell was going on in his mind? I asked myself, my body trembling and my breathing quickening. I could even see his eyes changing, something I thought wasn't going to happen.

I knew that he was a wolf shifter, so I was aware he could transform…

"Thanks. I know that it was weird what happened, but really… It doesn't really mean that I want to fuck you," I said, taking another step to the side and then finally moving away from him. I thought that Carwel was going to stop me, but he didn't. He let me walk away from there, and then I soon found myself in the classroom, everyone glancing at me as though they knew something had happened. But nobody did unless they could read my mind and know exactly what the change in my scent meant.

After sitting down, relief washed over me, but it only lasted a few seconds, my eyes soon finding Carwel walking behind the door, heading wherever he was going, his uniform complimenting him to perfection.

I mean, he was already perfect without his uniform, but with it on, he was even more mouthwatering.

I took a deep breath the moment when someone poked me on the shoulder from behind me, getting my attention.

"Hey, by any chance do you know how to solve this problem?"

He asked. I knew who he was, so it was a surprise to me that he was struggling with it. At least, I wasn't alone, I thought before teaching him everything that Carwel had taught me, which was actually a lot, opening a lot of doors for things that I thought I didn't quite understand.

After that, I took a deep rest while realizing that the worst was over and I could focus on what was going to happen from this moment onward.

If there was something that I was beginning to learn, it was that I didn't have to be afraid of everything all the time.

CHAPTER 7

Nokon

That was why I didn't stop myself before loading up my profile on ClickDesire, finding out that my match with Carwel was still there. What did I think was going to happen now? I asked myself, rolling over on the mattress before clicking on his profile one more time, and this time I found out that his photos weren't available.

What the hell? I asked myself, jamming my finger on the screen while trying not to freak out as much as I already was.

He couldn't have hidden his photos because of me, right? I asked myself, jamming my finger on the screen one more time, and then yet one more time, doing this so many times I thought I was going to break it. Thankfully, that didn't happen.

After jamming my finger on the screen for the final time, I stopped what I was doing before looking out the window, lowering my hand.

So, that happened, and I had no idea what to do now. It was obvious that me ghosting Carwel had that effect on me, an effect that I didn't want to think about. I didn't want to feel that I hurt him, even though that could be exactly what happened.

After sighing and thinking that it was all over, my phone buzzed, giving me some renewed hope, even though I didn't know what to do with it.

I turned on the screen of the phone one more time, seeing that there was indeed another notification. This time, it was a message from Carwel, and I'd been kind of expecting it to come.

No choice but to press my finger on it now.

Carwel: look, whatever happened today on campus, I want to say that I'm sorry about it.

He was sorry? I asked myself, for some reason not trying to believe that, even though it just made sense.

He was quite rude to me, after all.

Me: it's okay, I guess. You don't need to worry about it. I know that it was weird and rude, me ghosting you.

Carwel: good. Don't do that again. I'm surprised that you matched with me. To be honest, when I signed up for this dating app, I didn't think I was going to find anyone from college here, much less you. I didn't think that there was anyone in your age range interested in someone a little older like me.

A little older? I asked myself, chuckling. A little older was putting it mildly, but he wasn't going to say anything about it, especially now that we were already texting.

Me: I promise I'll never do that again.

Carwel: good. So, what are you doing now?

Me: I'm lying on my bed, bored as shit right now. And you?

Carwel: same. I'm trying to 'develop' a different recipe. Wanna see it?

I wasn't going to deny that I wanted to see it, though now that we matched, I was hoping we would be talking about something else which involved sending nudes. Still wasn't going to complain about it, though.

Again, the same problems from before persisted, and I couldn't just date someone so much older than me, considering all the repercussions that would follow it.

But what was the problem with texting him for a little bit right now? None. There was no problem with doing that, I thought, waiting for him to send me whatever it was that he was 'developing.'

I actually thought that he was going to send me a photo of what he was making on his stove, but it was actually just a photo of what he was writing on a piece of paper. What the hell? I asked myself, actually thinking that… It kind of made sense, considering Carvel's personality.

He did say that he was developing a different recipe, and the recipe that he was 'working on' was not like anything I had seen before, I thought, thinking more about that while sneaking my hand under my pants and stroking my dick.

Now that we were texting, I couldn't help but wonder if we could begin to talk about something else. My balls ached for that, after all.

Me: looks pretty tasty. Maybe you could make it for me sometime.
Carwel: I'll think about it.

After that, silence. Nothing coming from him, and I couldn't help but wonder why that was. We were just texting and having a good time, and considering that he was older, I had always thought that he should be the one to instigate the continuation of our chat.

Still, nada. I wondered what the hell was going on. Did he have a problem with hooking up with me? Maybe it was the age gap?

I didn't know, but I actually didn't have to worry too much about that, another message coming from him.

Carwel: feel comfortable sharing nudes with me?

After he asked me that, my eyes went wide, my heart stopping for a moment. After sitting up on the bed in a heartbeat, my mind went back and forth about what my answer should be.

I did want to share some nudes with him, but there were so many problems with that, thinking that I never thought that things between us would get so hot so soon.

CHAPTER 8

Carwel

After such a long time deciding who I should date, I thought that I finally found someone that was worth it. Again, I was telling myself I was only doing this because it was nothing more than a hookup. At least, that was what I kept hammering into my mind, hoping that nobody would ever find out about it, much less the people higher than me in the Alpha MC.

Nokon: I don't know if I should.

I didn't know if I should go on with this, but after taking that risk and initiating this path, I couldn't go back anymore. Still, I would feel like trash if I did it, I thought, my hand stroking my dick while thinking about him naked.

I couldn't help but wonder how his body looked without his clothes. Again, Nokon was the very definition of a twink, so I knew that he was mouthwatering. My shaft was already rock-hard thinking about it.

Me: well, we don't have to, but since we already know that there is a connection between us, I thought: why shouldn't we do it? Are you, maybe, telling me that you actually don't find me hot?

So, I threw that into the void between us. If he thought that there was nothing between us, then this was where it would all stop and I wouldn't go on.

Nokon: it's not really that. Actually, I do like you, quite a lot. It's just that you're so much older than me and I don't know if hooking up with you would be okay.

Ahh, so that was what was going on here, I thought. Well, I'd been thinking the same, but I didn't want to tell him that. This could still be a mistake, but it was making my dick so hard right now, thinking about stretching his sex so much that he would have difficulty walking.

My fur was already growing and showing, thinking about that.

Me: you don't have to make it weird if you don't think about it.

Nokon: hahaha as if it were so easy, but... alright. I guess I don't have to think about it so much.

Me: so... do you wanna see my dick or not?

I threw that into the void between us and I hoped that he was going to take the bait.

*Nokon: actually *unzips* I think that I'm going to take the initiative this time.*

And right after sending me that, a photo of his dick and balls came through, filling the screen of my phone. Fucking hell. It was appetizing. My mouth watered just looking at it, and now I couldn't help but wonder how I would feel if his dick was filling my mouth.

Well, I couldn't leave him hanging and thinking about my dick, so I unzipped too, and uploaded a photo of my prick.

There was silence, with me wondering if he liked it or not. I was pretty confident about it, so I wasn't anxious about his reaction. What I was anxious about was seeing more pictures of his shaft. It wasn't big, but it was still lust-inducing, the red gland swollen and already looking so ready to be devoured.

Nokon: makes me want to suck on it right away.

My heart beating a little faster than normal, I couldn't help but give him the invitation that he was looking for.

Me: well, you can come over. I don't bite, I promise :) Plus, we could even order pizza. I'm still working on that recipe that I'm developing, so you don't need to worry about eating anything that you don't want.

Nokon: actually, I would like to taste how good it is.

Me: I might be open for that another night, but for tonight, especially if you want it, we should go for something simple so that we can focus on ourselves.

My fingers moving around my balls, I hoped that he was going to say that he was going to come. We would only hook up, nothing more than that.

Nokon: right, I'm going now. Give me the address.

And I sent him my address, waiting for him to come over. After that, I exited the chat and took a shower, making sure that I looked my best and smelled nice to him.

Moments after that, I also cleaned up my apartment, which was where I lived. It wasn't too far from the campus, but it was close enough that I didn't have to drive for too long to go there.

Taking another look around my apartment, I sprayed air freshener in the rooms, and then sat on the couch in the living room while waiting for Nokon to come. I told the reception desk that he could come up here without them having to call me, and they told me that there was no problem with that.

So, at this point, I was just waiting for Nokon to shoot me a message on the phone, telling me that he had already reached the premises.

While I was idly browsing some web pages on my phone, I heard the doorbell chime. That was him, I thought, shooting up from the couch and already going to the door. I opened it and I found him just standing there, wearing a nice, plain black shirt and a pair of dark jeans, looking even nicer now and more assured of himself than all the times I'd seen him on campus.

My dick growing under my pants, it was very difficult for me not to devour him right away, but I still contained myself. Kept my urges in check even though his scent was pushing all the right buttons in me.

CHAPTER 9

Nokon

"Here, try this," he said, putting it into my mouth. It was a chocolate ball, which he made just for me. My tongue swirling around it, I salivated it and basked myself in it, enjoying the taste as much as I could before it melted.

After I stepped inside his apartment, we began to chat a little about ourselves, just enjoying each other's presence, trying to maneuver through this without it feeling too awkward.

To be honest, I was dealing with this a lot better than I'd thought I was going to. Carwel knew what he was doing, how to push all the right buttons, always making sure that I felt that he was paying attention to everything I needed.

In the meantime, I just couldn't stop glancing down and stealing glances at his crotch, thinking about his cock. Oh, I was thinking about so much more than that, imagining him putting it into my mouth and doing amazing things with it, and it was such a pity that I couldn't do so right now.

After melting the chocolate ball in my mouth, I swiped my finger over my bottom lip, still enjoying the taste of the chocolate for as long as possible while my eyes remained locked with his.

Carwel didn't make the recipe that he showed me before, but he still bought this chocolate box, whose quality and brand showed me just how much this moment meant to him. It couldn't be any different, I thought, my dick growing harder under my pants.

Before coming here, I made sure that I put on my best clothes and sprayed on my best perfume. Still, I couldn't help but wonder if he didn't prefer only smelling my scent. Carwel didn't say anything about that, so I wasn't going to bring it up.

While he was moving his hand back to himself, my hand brushed on his, making me feel tingles of pleasure through my entire body, wondering what else was going on in his mind.

His eyes were glazed over slightly, making me feel that he was full of lust as much as I was. He didn't attempt to move his hand away after touching mine, which assured me that he was enjoying this as much as I was, most likely thinking about fucking me right now.

But we were going to take it slow, especially because we didn't want to rush. Not to mention that I was a virgin and completely inexperienced, and I didn't want to do anything that could spook me.

"So, did you like it?" He asked, his voice gentle and powerful at the same time. It reverberated in the air, making me feel tingles of excitement.

"Yeah, but I still would have preferred if you made it yourself. After showing me that recipe and that you were working on it, I thought that's exactly what you were going to do. I thought that you were going to cook something for me and was going to show me how good of a cook you are."

He chuckled, putting his hand on my thigh all of a sudden and without giving me any sign that he was going to do that. To be honest, it was difficult for me to complain about it, so I just let it happen, enjoying the weight of it on me.

After stepping into his apartment and chatting for a little while longer with him, it was pretty obvious that we were going to fuck.

We just didn't know who would take the first step, but considering my inexperience and that he was older than me - again my mind just brought that up as if it were bigger than it was.

Now… Now just might be the right time to kiss him.

His eyes still holding me, his pupils slightly dilating, his scent growing thicker and more prevalent, I couldn't help but wonder when it was going to happen when he was finally going to show me that he wanted me much more than anything or anyone else.

His hand slid up, approaching my crotch. Sighing, I couldn't help but bask in the warmth coming from my body, growing stronger with each second, his hand feeling heavier on my thigh.

Carwel leaned down slightly, making me wonder again if he was going to kiss me right now, everything happening at a snail's pace.

The box of chocolate sat on the coffee table, forgotten for the time being. Even though the chocolate was excellent and it just melted on my tongue right after the first contact, I wasn't thinking about it. I wasn't thinking about its strong flavor, my mind focused on me kissing him.

His lips looked so plump, my mind remembering that I hadn't thought that I would ever kiss the guard who worked on my college campus.

They were a little closer to me now. His lips parted slightly, making me think that he was going to kiss me, but then he just stopped. Blinking, I couldn't help but wonder what was going on in his mind, but it wasn't like I could read it. Such a pity, wishing that it was different.

The heat emanating from his body bathed me in it, making sweat drops come from the pores in my skin, my heart rate picking up. If this didn't result in him kissing me, I didn't know what would do that.

My mouth felt dry, his hand still going up on my thigh. Everything was tense and there was this feeling that whatever was happening now couldn't be stopped anymore.

Then, it was all impossible to control, and we just sealed our lips together, and it was the best moment of my life and also when I finally lost the virginity of my mouth.

I would never forget it, I thought, just putting my arms over his shoulders and bringing him closer to me, feeling his body pressing against mine while he brought himself down on me, pinning me onto the couch.

After that, it was so easy for him to dominate me, his hands going under my shirt, feeling my skin. As he did that, I felt aftershocks of pleasure in my body, my dick hard in an instant, everything about this begging for me to open my legs for him.

CHAPTER 10

I still couldn't believe that this was happening, his hands everywhere on my body, feeling every part of me, every inch, dominating me. After throwing my legs around his lower back, I made sure I was the one pinning him down and that he couldn't move anymore, much less think about ending our kiss no matter what went on.

We kissed for what felt like an eternity and when breathing became difficult, I could feel how tense his muscles were, his body begging for more of me.

"That was amazing," I said, breathless. I didn't lie. It was just amazing and I wanted so much more of it.

"You were amazing," he confessed, showing me that he didn't lie about that, just wishing that we were doing so much more.

After that, silence. I couldn't help but wonder what was going on in his mind, and I didn't have to wonder much more when he snuck his hand under my pants, looking for my dick. Finding it, he started to stroke it slowly and carefully, focusing his fingers on my gland.

Groaning and moaning, I thought that I was going to come then and there, but I didn't. I wasn't going to show my inexperience, especially not so soon.

As if to show me that he wasn't quite yet done with me, he

kissed me one more time, and this time he made sure that it was much more passionate than before, his tongue going into my mouth, digging in and looking for dominance, which he found in such a short amount of time it was overwhelming.

Again, I was breathless and huffing, his hands moving all over my body while focusing on my nipples.

When Carwel broke the kiss again, he took off my shirt. I had little time to react to that, moving my arms up so that I helped him. When he was done, his eyes went up and down, feasting on what they were seeing.

"I knew that you are beautiful, but I never thought it was so breathtaking," he murmured, his fingers enjoying and twirling my nipples gently, showing how much this moment meant.

Now that he was mounted on me, his dick rubbed and pressed on me, instigating waves of pleasure through my body. I could only think about one thing, which was to take his dick in my hand and love it with my fingers.

When would it happen? I asked myself, so hard and hot right now, thinking about the size of his dick and how it would feel in my hand.

"Well, are you going to leave me wondering if I can say the same about you?" I teased, my hand stroking his skin gently, drawing small circles on his back. Even through his shirt, I could feel it, basking myself in it.

He leaned off me, his hands going under his shirt before lifting it. Seeing his chest for the first time was nothing short of mouthwatering, and I found myself hornier than before, something I didn't think possible. After that, I pushed myself up on my elbows, my hands going for his body, gliding all over it and exploring every inch, cherishing his hard muscles.

"Of course I'm not going to leave you wondering about that," he murmured, getting off of me. I stood up and he helped me take off my pants, his hands sliding over my thighs, cupping my bulge. Massaging it, he made me moan and groan, my dick harder now than it had ever been.

After that, he put his fingers under my pair of boxer briefs, lowering them down. His mouth salivated, his eyes feasting on my rod standing proud and erect in front of him. Carwel knew what he wanted, and he was going to get exactly that.

But it wasn't what I wanted, so I put my hand on his shoulder and told him to stand back up. After he did that, I went on my knees, Carwel stepping out of his pants.

Moments later, I helped him take off his pair of boxer briefs, finding his mesmerizing, hypnotizing cock. It was bigger now than I had thought possible, veins protruding and pulsing, his goal just one right now – which was to fuck me until nothing was left of me.

After that realization dawned on me, I licked my lips, my fingers going around his girth. Him being circumcised meant that I didn't have much skin to play with, which was kind of expected and disappointing, though it was really slight and it didn't bother me at all.

My mind was actually focused on something else. His big, gargantuan dick pointing right at my mouth, and I couldn't help but lick my lips, stroking it, the movement of my hand slow and methodical, wishing to drag this for as long as possible.

Finally, I was going to give head for the first time, and I couldn't help but wonder how I was going to feel and if my inexperience was going to show. I hoped that it wasn't going to, but I couldn't know that for sure.

My hand was shaking slightly, and I was surprised when Carwel grabbed it. Looking up, my eyes found his, and I couldn't help but wonder what he was going to say. When he parted his lips, though, I knew that it was going to be exactly what I needed to go on without more anxiety impeding me from doing my best.

"I know that this is your first time, and I know that you need to take your time with it. Don't worry about me and what I'm going to do when you are running your tongue on my dick - I know it's going to be amazing."

And those were exactly the words I needed to hear to go on, so I didn't waste any time, stroking his dick a couple more times before finally diving my head, putting his gland between my lips, and enjoying it for everything it was.

Just to make sure that I wasn't going to be overwhelmed by this, he settled his hand on the back of my head.

Carwel wasn't dictating the pace, but he kept it there to make sure that nothing he didn't want happened. It was his way to maintain control over me.

CHAPTER 11

Still sliding my tongue around his cockhead, I felt invigorated, soon doing everything he wanted when I realized that this was under my control and sucking him off wasn't as hard as I thought it was going to be.

Pre-come seeping out of the slit, I found myself so empowered by this I didn't know what was going to happen, just that I was enjoying this far too much not to continue with it. After that, it was so easy for me, still playing with his nuts and dancing my fingers between them, taking as much time as I thought it was going to take, his body hot and sweaty. After what felt like an eternity, he pushed me off of him, making me wonder what was going on in his mind right now. I looked up, then he let me dive my head between his legs again, taking his shaft into my mouth one more time.

"Thought it was over?" He asked, his eyes feasting on me while he smirked. "It's far from over. In fact, this is only the beginning."

Hearing that, I couldn't help but feel immense pleasure overflowing from me, enjoying this moment so much more that I just had to continue worshiping his shaft, sliding my tongue around his cockhead, my fingers still dancing with his nuts. They were laden with his milk, and I could only wonder when he was going to cum into my mouth.

Actually, now that I was showing myself to be so slutty, I couldn't help but wonder when he would shoot his come into my hole.

My body begged for that.

After playing with his scrotum for what felt like an eternity and worshiping his manhood, I finally pulled my head back when I felt I'd had enough. Following that, Carwel took my hand and made me stand up.

"Let me return the favor," he announced before getting on his knees. What he thought he was going to do before, he was going to do now. After encasing my rod with his fingers, he gave it a couple of strokes, dragging this moment for as long as he could, his eyes watering.

I couldn't help but take a step back, his fingers still doing something so amazing I never thought it possible. My body was pulsing with his rhythm, his fingers still working my gland while showing his experience.

I could imagine doing this many more times in the future with him, but... I still didn't want to make any promises.

Moving away from me, he stopped right when it was the best moment. Carwel stopped when I thought I was going to come into his mouth, which would have been amazing.

"Just got you into the right mood, so I think that now I want to take this where you can feel more comfortable," he promised, putting his hand on my shoulder and making me moonwalk into his bedroom. Kicking the door closed behind him, he threw me onto his bed, lunging at me.

With Carwel on top of me now after landing on the mattress, he could do everything and anything he wanted, his body shadowing me. The light coming from the ceiling bulb went around him and my eyes could barely make out his face. I could see his eyes and they were hungry with only one goal right now, which was to pleasure me as much as he could.

Back to being my old self, shyness overtook me again, his hands loving and cherishing me, still doing everything he wanted. Moments later, he turned me around and then made me go on all fours, his body language showing me exactly what he was going to do, which was to penetrate me.

My ass up and exposed, shivers ran down my spine. I was thinking that, after he slammed his prick inside of me, it was going to be difficult for me to go to college and attend all the classes I needed to without signaling to other people that something happened to me the night before.

But if people began to ask me questions about that, I would have to deflect all of them. No other way around it.

Just after that, the sound of something being ripped in the bedroom warned my ears, making me turn my head around so that I could look over my shoulder, wondering what he was doing. It took me a little time to find out that he was putting on a condom, something I was going to admit made me feel some disappointment.

But I understood why he was doing this. Carwel wasn't going to knock me up no matter how much he wanted me and no matter how much the mere sight of me under him stoked his horniness levels.

After turning my head back around, I gripped the bedsheets, making sure that no matter how this happened and no matter how much pain he inflicted on me, I was going to hold on.

Moments later, Carwel plunged his prick deep inside of me, breaking every barrier while instigating waves of pain in my body. My eyes almost rolled inside my head and I thought I was going to pass out, but I didn't.

It was too much, and from that moment onward it was bliss, his body pistoning in and out of me. I came, shooting my cum all over the bedsheets. My mind was in such a daze of different, conflicting and yet mixing thoughts right now that I didn't want to think about how much of an asshole I was being by staining his bedsheets with my load.

But it was true that Carwel didn't mind that, unloading his milk in the condom until he finally stopped rolling his hips after climbing down from his orgasmic high.

Some moments after that, he lied down on the bed with

me and cocooned me in his arms. I didn't worry about falling asleep, my mind thinking that, since he lived close to the college's campus, he could take me there without it being a hassle to him.

Closing my eyes and with him spooning me, that was precisely what I was thinking about while I fell asleep.

Just after that, he murmured something into my ear, but my mind was so tired, as was my body, that I couldn't think about anything.

I just fell asleep.

CHAPTER 12

Holding the box in my hand, the only thing I was thinking about now, after going out on so many nights with Nokon, was that this moment just felt right.

I was planning on making this afternoon much different than anything we'd had before. We'd pushed past the age gap issue, meaning that we didn't talk about it anymore, even though sometimes I knew that it popped back up into his mind.

He was inside his house and I was standing on the porch, wondering when he was going to open the door. Feeling some anxiety, I knew he was going to do it. Nokon was probably in his bedroom sleeping when I showed up here.

The position of the sun and the slow traffic around here meant that it was early in the morning. Given his classes and that his major was hard, last night he had to have been studying for hours on end without taking a break.

Still, I was already rocking back and forth on my heels, my fingers tapping on the gift-wrapped box.

It was a gift, a gift that was going to bring a different shine to his eyes.

Just after I raised my hand, preparing myself to knock on the door, he opened it. Rubbing his eyes with his hands, Nokon yawned.

"Good morning, sleepyhead," I jested, stepping into his house without waiting for an invitation, which was common between us now, considering that this was far from the first time that I was visiting his house.

"Good morning. What are you doing here so early?" He questioned, still rubbing his eyes. Looking at him up and down, I noticed that he was wearing his pajamas, which were light blue, his favorite color.

Seeming so cute right now, I just wanted to rip his pajamas off of him, but I wasn't going to do that, even though my body was begging me to do it.

When his eyes noticed what I was holding, he asked, "what's that?"

"It's a gift. I hope you're going to like it."

"A gift?" he asked, padding over to me. His hands sliding on the box and checking it, he finally found the lace, which he pulled and undid in the next few seconds.

My hands still trembled while he opened the box, in a couple of seconds finding out what was in it. After that, Nokon found what he was looking for, holding it between his hands.

Some weeks ago, he told me that he had always wanted this, but that given his lack of money and the fact that his parents never gave him enough, he never had the opportunity to buy it.

Even now, he was still rubbing his eyes, wondering what he was seeing.

"Am I really looking at this?" He asked, whirling around and accelerating to the window so that he could see the item better.

Inside that box, there was – or there had been – another box, which he was now turning in his hands over and over again, wondering if he was in a dream or if this was real life.

"I told you about it before, but I never thought that you were going to buy it for me," he confessed, turning around and smiling broadly.

"Well, I just wanted to surprise you. Looks like it's working."

Growing up, Nokon never had the opportunity to buy a drone and, now that he had classes, he couldn't save enough money for it, one of the reasons why he had always been postponing this purchase.

I wasn't rich, but I was his boyfriend, thinking about the possibility of him being the one, which was why I wanted to give him this drone, which he could already turn on and begin to play with in his backyard. His neighbors were probably going to be pissed by the noise and it flying above their houses, but there was nothing they could do about it.

Now that Nokon was grinning so much, he could do everything and anything he wanted.

"This is amazing," he exclaimed before rushing into the backyard. I held up my hand, trying to stop him, but it was pointless. The moment he was outside, he ripped the box open and began to play with the drone.

Putting my hand on his shoulder, I made him turn around, his eyes glistening with joy.

"I... *love you.* I want to make this permanent. I want you to come live with me, and maybe one day we won't have to hide our relationship from anyone anymore. What do you think? Do you want it, too?"

Dropping the controller, he froze up for a moment, and I could only wonder what he was thinking. Fearing that he was going to show me that he didn't expect that from me and that we should break up, I thought that he was going to start yelling at me, but he didn't.

"I love you too, and I... think that's a fantastic idea."

CHAPTER 13

Carwel

Nokon lived with me now. I never thought it would happen, but now that we entered a different phase in our lives, everything was even more perfect than before, the smell of barbecue wafting in the air while it impregnated my lungs.

About telling other people about us... I didn't know if and when it would ever happen, but the more time that we spent together, it became something that I kept on thinking about, wondering when I would finally shatter that fear.

Nokon was the one at the barbecue grill, flipping the burgers. Now that I was seeing this, he was quite good at it, something that never crossed my mind before.

I wasn't feeling down, but there was that issue that kept popping back up in my mind so many times, always wondering when I would muster up enough courage to ask him about it.

Flipping another burger, his eyes shifted to me, most likely wondering what the hell was going on in my mind. We brought some friends over, so they were around him, chatting with him, but every so often, I noticed that he looked at me, wondering what I was thinking and why I was seated on this bench, hunched over.

I was holding something in my hand. It was a photo. A portrait, to be more precise, which showed the day after he told me he loved me.

It was at that moment I realized that we could have an amazing life together. People thought that we were just friends, but they didn't know that we were actually much more than that.

The sun was bright in the sky, shining on me. I took a deep breath, standing up before going to the front of the house. When I said that we would live together, I decided that we should live in his house. It just made more sense, considering how spacious it was.

My apartment was a temporary place, and I never intended on living there for the rest of my life. That was what I was thinking, anyway, wishing that he would just come over to me and ask me what was going on.

Just before I reached the front of the house, I did notice that he'd taken off his apron, rushing over to me. This being a nice party where we were kicking back and enjoying this moment while bonding with his family, I didn't want to ruin anything, but... I supposed that now it was too late.

Nokon stopped in front of me and I leaned on the wall behind me. Looking down at him, I couldn't help but wonder how I was going to weigh my words.

After all, I had to be careful.

"What's going on?" He asked, his voice echoing his disbelief and how much he thought that he never imagined I wasn't going to be enjoying today as much as I should be. "You look worried about something, and I can't help but wonder why."

I took a deep breath. I thought that it was going to be much harder for me to convince myself that we should disclose to everyone about our relationship, but his family was big on him finding the right Alpha, which made me think that he didn't want to tell them anything unless he was sure about it.

"There's something we need to talk about."

"Don't tell me it's about that same thing you keep bringing up."

"It's about that, yes."

He ran his hand over his face.

"How many times do I have to tell you that it will only happen when I'm ready for it?"

"Doing that only makes it all worse. I think that the more we continue to hide it, the worse it will be when everyone here finds out the truth."

"Nobody will find out anything."

"You don't know that. They are probably already asking themselves why I have my stuff here and it looks like I sleep here after we told them that we are not in a relationship."

"They don't have to think about anything. They are happy. They are smiling and have even congratulated me on my midterm scores."

I chuckled, stepping away from him. It all bugged me so much, and I just wanted to do something about it and bury it for good.

"That's what you think, but we all know it's not so simple."

"You don't know anything about that. You are just making a mountain out of a molehill."

I shook my head, tsking. I had really thought that Nokon could better understand where I was coming from with this, but the way that he just said that infuriated me. I had thought that he was truly interested in understanding my reasons and thoughts, but after living with him for these last months, I began to see that he was more selfish than I'd assumed he was. He was more selfish when it came to his thoughts and wishes. Sometimes, he remembered that I had those too, but he always made everything about himself, one of the reasons why we were growing more distant.

"You're leaving?" He asked, sounding dumbfounded. Of course I was leaving. This place was toxic, though I did imagine myself coming back here in the next couple of hours when my head was clearer about what I should do.

In the end, our relationship was the most important thing in the world to me and I would never risk it, no matter how much all of this infuriated me.

"I just need some space," I grumbled before getting onto my motorcycle and putting on my helmet. Turning the engine on, I rode off while checking the mirrors, seeing Nokon just standing outside, staring at me as though he couldn't believe that this was happening.

After all, he thought that it was all sunshine and rainbows between us, but now I realized that it wasn't so simple.

We both wanted the same thing. The only problem was that I realized that I wanted it way sooner. Could I wait until he was ready? I could, but I also realized that it could be something that he would always continue postponing, never facing it head-on, which was a deal breaker to me.

CHAPTER 14

Carwel

Coming back home, I knew that it was going to be a mess, so much so that I couldn't help but sigh. This was a mess that I didn't want to face head-on, even though it was contradictory, considering my previous statements and thoughts about it.

I didn't want to face it head-on, thinking about what Nokon was probably obsessing over right now. He thought that my reasons were bullshit, but it was actually his inability to understand me that was getting on my nerves, always thinking that he would rather keep our relationship hidden no matter how bad it was to us.

I took a few steps toward the bedroom. Our bedroom, I remembered. There were so many amazing memories associated with it, and every time I thought about it, I remembered us loving each other under the blanket.

The truth was, after everything that we did and went through, I began to think that we were actually meant for each other. I started to suspect that we were fated mates. We could never know that until it was the right time, and now I thought it was.

I took a deep breath in, opening the door before finding out that my Omega wasn't in the room. What the hell? I asked myself, rushing into every room in the house and finding out that he was in none of them.

Getting desperate, I headed outside where the grill was, but I still didn't find him there, which made me feel so desperate I thought I would freak out.

He never did this to me. Not before, anyway. Every time that I came back home, he was always somewhere in the house, more often than not either in the living room or in the bedroom.

I took a deep breath in, pulling out my phone and checking for his status. He wasn't online, which could mean many things, but to me, it meant he went somewhere else, a place where he didn't have to be thinking about anything – not anything that bothered him and made him feel as though he couldn't see things clearly.

It was the only place where I knew he could've gone.

So, I just hopped onto my motorcycle, riding off there. The wind blowing on my face, I couldn't wait until I was within sight distance and I could see his legs dangling from the edge, his eyes contemplating the trains coming and going below him.

His eyes spotted me before I got there, so I knew that this moment was going to be much more stressful and defining than I thought it was going to be.

After hopping off my motorcycle, I climbed up the path to get to him. Sitting down next to his side, I said, "I know what I said before hurt you, so I just want to say that I'm sorry about it. If you want to take your time telling everyone about our relationship, I suppose it's fine with me."

Still, it wasn't what I wanted. It was difficult for me, thinking about it all the time, imagining when I would finally tell my friends and family the good news.

He took a deep breath, finding my hand and grabbing it. Sighing, he said, "I think it's fine. I think that we should finally tell everyone about us, now that I know how shitty it is to be hiding it from so many people while thinking that it's fine. One day, they will find out the truth anyway."

Looking at his eyes, I couldn't help but feel so certain about it. I never thought it would happen, but now that he was holding me with his gaze, his eyes slightly teary, I could tell he'd been thinking about it the whole day.

After dissecting all possible repercussions, he finally came to a decision. When it came to setting his mind on something, he wasn't good at it, something that I'd always found kind of funny.

"You sure? I don't want to do it without your okay."

"Yeah, I'm sure. It's exactly what I want, thinking about us. I overreacted before. I overreacted thinking that you were going to leave me, so that's why I came here. Watching the trains go and come below me helps me think, so I just want to make that clear."

After he said that, I hugged him, throwing my arms around his body while pressing it tightly into mine. The heat of his body bathed me in it, and it also warmed my heart.

"Thank you. I knew that you were going to understand how much this means to me. It took me so much to work up the courage to tell the Alpha MC about us, so it means a lot that you understand my reasons."

After kissing me one more time, he said, "and how are you going to reward me for making the choice you wanted?"

Smirking, I knew what he wanted, so I wasted no time before taking his hand and standing up with him. After that, we went to my motorcycle, sitting on it.

After putting on my helmet, I said, "I'm going to reward you by claiming you in our bed, like so many other times where I had you."

Putting his arms around me and tightening them, he said, "You've just read my thoughts. I can't wait until you are loving me the only way you can."

NOKON'S EPILOGUE

It was difficult for me, waiting in the living room while everyone stared at me, most likely wondering what the hell was going to happen now. To be honest, I was impatient, tapping my foot on the floor while waiting for Carwel to come back from the college's campus.

Everyone, including my family and friends, and even his own family was here. We were all waiting for him to come back, the clock ticking behind me with painful beats. Never before had my mind been struck by so much anxiety as now, with me feeling as though the ground was going to open up and swallow me whole.

"Are you sure he is coming? You've told us before that he is only your friend, so I don't understand why we have to wait for him."

"Don't worry, he's going to come. Before we all begin to pluck the hair off our heads, he'll be here," I assured my father, who shifted on the couch, sighing and shaking his head.

His opinion of Carwel would soon change when he realized that he was someone respectable.

Taking a deep breath, I tapped my foot on the floor one more time the moment the rumbling noise of his motorcycle in the distance informed me that he just arrived.

I rushed over to the door before opening it and finding him pulling up in the driveway. Hopping off the motorcycle, he took off his helmet. After that, he entered the house with me and I did something I thought I never would when my family and friends were around.

They all even perked up, their eyes going wide while wondering what was going on here.

I looked at him, saying, "there's something fundamental that I need to say, and I don't know how to word it, so I'm just going to be blunt: Carwel isn't just my friend. He's my mate. We've been together for a long time now and I think it's time I finally told you the truth." I took a deep breath before saying, "he's my boyfriend and I love him. I want to be with him for the rest of my life. That's the reason why I gathered all of you here, and I want you to accept us."

What did I suspect was going to happen now? I asked myself, not knowing the answer to that question, especially with everyone just staring back at us, everything seeming as though it was frozen in time.

"Actually, we've been wondering this whole time when you would finally tell us the truth," my father confessed, rising to his feet and holding out his hand to greet the person who could become my husband. "Congratulations! I know that we don't know each other well yet, but I think that you could be an excellent partner for my son."

Joy growing in me, I didn't know how to take this. It started better than I thought, and then when everybody else began to share their opinions, I knew I made the right choice.

CARWEL'S EPILOGUE

"No, you are supposed to do it this way," I explained, positioning myself by his side while putting his hands on the handlebars, making sure that he didn't apply too much force. Tek was learning how to ride his first motorcycle, sitting on it.

As for me, I wasn't going to retire, but I was moving up to another rank. It was better than my previous one and gave me a lot more reputation and responsibility.

"Yes, boss," he said, his voice echoing his self-esteem, his eyes focused on this.

In the meantime, Nokon was in the distance, flicking his tongue at the ice cream cone he held in his hand. Sitting on my motorcycle, he looked so lovely that I just wanted to go there right away, and it was a pity that I couldn't, having to make sure that Trek learned everything he needed to learn first.

He twisted the ignition of the motorcycle, smiling when the engine came to life. With the engine rumbling underneath him, I could tell that he was beginning to pick up some of the tips I gave him.

"I think I've got it, boss," he said, trying to make the motorcycle go forward, but then the engine just died. I chuckled, covering my mouth.

"Don't worry about it. You are going to get the hang of it soon," I promised, unfolding my arms from my chest before turning around and going to Nokon, who was waiting for me after finishing his ice cream cone.

I reached him a moment later, grabbing his hand and holding it while pulling him off the motorcycle and away from it. After that, I took him to the edge of the cliff, where we could admire the horizon. The sun setting in the distance, never before did I feel so complete, warmth rushing into my heart.

He turned to me, his eyes holding me.

Putting his arms around my lower waist, he said, "I love you so much and, every time I think about you, it is only strengthened."

After pecking his lips, I said, "I love you too so much and I want you to know that. You are the one that I always wanted to be with, the one that has always been meant to be with me."

Hearing that, he didn't even seem surprised, just knowing that it was always the case and that it couldn't be any different.

While hearing Tek trying to make the motorcycle start again, we kissed one more time while the sun bathed us with its warm, inviting colors.

We were meant for each other.

The End

Looking for the first two books in the series? Find them here:

1. Omega's Possessive Alpha
2. Alpha's Surrogate Omega

The next page also contains a teaser for book 1.
And don't forget to leave your review. It really helps me!

TEASER: OMEGA'S POSSESSIVE ALPHA

MPREG Wolf Shifter Romance (Alpha MC - 1)

Look, it didn't really matter how much my father wanted to make this happen, it wasn't going to. Even though the party was energetic, it wasn't going to make me fall for the cocky guy standing across from me all the way on the other side of the main hall.

"He's just so much older than me. There is no way that there can ever be a relationship between us," I said to my best friend. Draco was standing here with me and he was a member of the pack.

Even though I would never say this, the truth was that I would rather be in a romantic relationship with him than with Lux. I mean, it just wouldn't really work.

Although, I couldn't help but admit that he was quite the eye candy. He was fit. His body was sculpted, his muscles showing even though he was wearing a dark suit. It didn't really fit him, though. I just had no idea what he even thought he was doing here at this party.

"Does age really matter that much? I mean, he is only 30 years old and you are 21. It's about time you started to go to college or just do something with your life. I'm in college, and I really enjoy it."

Draco tried to smile, but he wasn't really fooling anyone here. He didn't actually enjoy attending classes and whatever else he thought he was doing in college. As for me, my career was focused on something else. I was focused on becoming a developer. A programmer. That was what I was focused on and nothing would change that.

I took a sip from the wineglass I was holding. Grimacing, I just really couldn't understand why people thought that wine tasted good. It just didn't.

"It matters to me. I'm not going to begin a relationship with anyone just because my father wants it. Not to mention that he still thinks there is something as ridiculous as 'fated mates.' Just thinking about it, I feel like I'm going to puke."

And yet, my eyes couldn't stop glancing to the left and stealing glances at him. I had no idea what I was even doing. If Lux noticed that I was stealing glances at him, he would certainly take the next step and come to me.

"I just think that you are wrong about this. You should go and talk to him at least. It can't really hurt," he said as he winked. I rolled my eyes and then began to walk away. Where to? I didn't know. Anywhere that wasn't the main hall was good enough for me.

In a moment, I found myself outside, and here I could breathe and think about everything going on in my life. There was this pressure on me to marry and find my partner, even though it was ridiculous.

I sat down on a chair by the swimming pool. I couldn't deny that I was spoiled. My house was more like a mansion. It was big and fancy, and I knew a lot of people would give almost everything they had to live the rest of their lives here.

At least, that was what I was telling myself anyway. I was just trying to make myself feel better about my current, shitty situation.

The air around me was fresh and calming. I inhaled it slowly while still thinking about Lux. What was about him that kept on making my mind go back to him all the time?

Maybe it was his impossibly blue eyes and his manly scent. I was an Omega, so I could smell him without difficulty even from a distance, just like now. Even though he was still in the main hall, I could smell him. And it was really like he was right behind me.

"I saw you coming here," his voice echoed behind me. I shot up from where I was sitting while whirling around and meeting his eyes as they continued to stare at me. I never thought that he would show up all of a sudden when I was trying to think about anything that didn't involve him.

"What are you doing here?" I asked as I raised my voice. It was like I was begging for someone to help me. Maybe Draco would come, but I didn't think so. He was probably mingling with the other partygoers right now.

"I needed some fresh air, so I came outside. Nothing more than that, really. It certainly doesn't mean that I wanted to talk to you in person." He smirked after saying that. Of course he was going to do that. Lux was so convinced about the effect he was having on me.

I took a few steps away from him. He wasn't going to fool me now no matter what happened.

"Stay away from me!" I shouted. This time, I did that while hoping that at least one of the partygoers would hear it. Whether that would happen or not, we were going to find out in the next couple of seconds.

But... There was only gentle music coming from the main hall. Nobody heard anything, which made me feel even more paralyzed than I was right now.

My cock was hard. There was no denying it. If there was something I wanted to make happen right now, it was this Alpha manhandling me the way that I knew he could. He would put me right back in my place and then he would kiss me. I could just imagine how soft his lips were.

But I shouldn't even be thinking that. He could read my mind. I was certain he could do that.

He lifted his hands and put them in front of him as though he was making a stop sign. "All right, all right. You don't need to worry about that. I'm not going to do anything to you that you don't want."

After a moment of silence, I realized that he wasn't going to harm me or try to touch me without my consent. Where was everybody? I asked myself, realizing how stupid I was being about this. The truth was that I was still in my house and, given that, Lux had to get out of here if I said so to the guards.

MPREG SERIES AND MORE

SERIES - OMEGAVERSE MC

1. Omega for Obsessive Alpha
2. Omega for Protective Alpha
3. Omega for Jealous Alpha

SERIES - PREGNANT FOR HIM

1. Controlled by the Alpha 1: An MPREG Omegaverse Story
2. Controlled by the Alpha 2: An MPREG Omegaverse Story
3. Controlled by the Alpha 3: Dominating the Fertile Omega
4. Controlled by the Alpha 4: An Omega's Tale of Obedience
5. Controlled by the Alpha 5: A Tale of Obedient Submission
6. Controlled by the Alpha 6: Monopolized in Outer Space

SERIES - LOST INNOCENCE

1. Overwhelming the Omega 1: His Little Doll
2. Overwhelming the Omega 2: Brute Entry and Double Teamed
3. Overwhelming the Omega 3: His Tight Backdoor
4. Overwhelming the Omega 4: Stretching his Front Door
5. Overwhelming the Omega 5: Until he Spasms
6. Overwhelming the Omega 6: Naïve and Untouched

ABOUT THE AUTHOR

Steamy MM stories, baby! Michael Levi can't go a day without sitting down and putting into words all the dirty scenes that sprout in his mind. His collection is diverse, but it's gay love only. And if you are looking for something free, check his mailing list. Warning: it can be extra spicy.

When Michael Levi isn't writing, he's chilling out by the lake close to his house. Nothing better than kicking back with a martini in his hand as he daydreams his next explicit scenes.